IMAGINE THAT™

Licensed exclusively to Imagine That Publishing Ltd
Tide Mill Way, Woodbridge, Suffolk, IP12 1AP, UK
www.imaginethat.com
Copyright © 2019 Imagine That Group Ltd
All rights reserved
2 4 6 8 9 7 5 3 1
Manufactured in China

Written by Carrie Hennon
Illustrated by Barbara Bakos

ISBN 978-1-78700-903-5

A catalogue record for this book is available from the British Library

For Mila Beau Eve Hennon.

I can't BEAR it!

Written by Carrie Hennon

Illustrated by Barbara Bakos

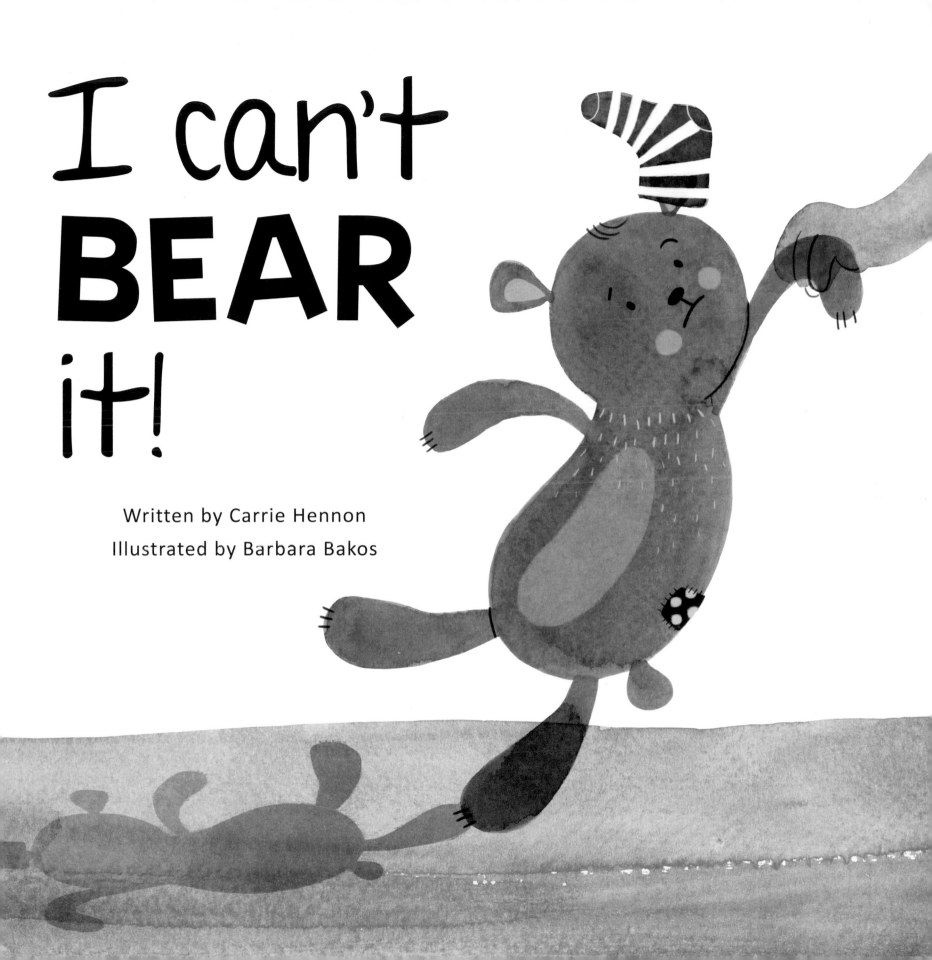

This is

Clare.

She might look like a sweet little girl ...

... but sometimes she can be a real

GRUMP!

This is

Bear.

When Clare doesn't want to do something she yells,

'I can't BEAR it!'

That's when Bear steps in.

'BEEP! BEEP! BEEP!' went the alarm.
It was time to get ready for school.

'I can't BEAR it!' groaned Clare.
'I'd rather stay in bed.'

'First position please girls,'

said the ballet teacher, as the dance class began.

'I can't BEAR it!' complained Clare.
'I'd rather fly my kite.'

'Screech! Screech! SCREECH!'
went the violins in the music lesson.

'I can't BEAR it!'

yelled Clare.
'I'd rather listen to my own kind of music.'

'Lunch is ready!'

called Dad,
as he put a bowl of crunchy green salad on the table.

'I can't BEAR it!' moaned Clare.
'I'd rather eat a big slice of pizza.'

'On your marks,
get set, GO!'

started the three-legged
race on sports day.

'I can't BEAR it!' huffed Clare.

'I'd rather hang upside down from a tree.'

Finish

When Mum asked Clare to tidy her room,
all Clare heard was, 'Blah, blah, blah!'

'I can't BEAR it!' sighed Clare.

'I'd rather play video games.'

'Come on Clare, it's time to help with the washing up,' called Mum.

'I can't BEAR it!'
grumbled Clare.
'I'd rather watch cartoons.'

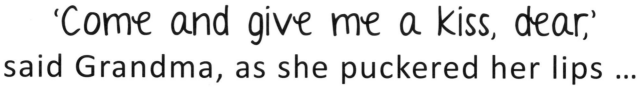

'Come and give me a kiss, dear,'
said Grandma, as she puckered her lips ...

'I can't BEAR it!' shrieked Clare.
'I'd rather kiss the dog.'

And so things continued …

Every time Clare didn't want to do something,
poor Bear had to take her place.

'BEAR?!'

Until one day, Bear was nowhere to be found ...

Getaway
Airways

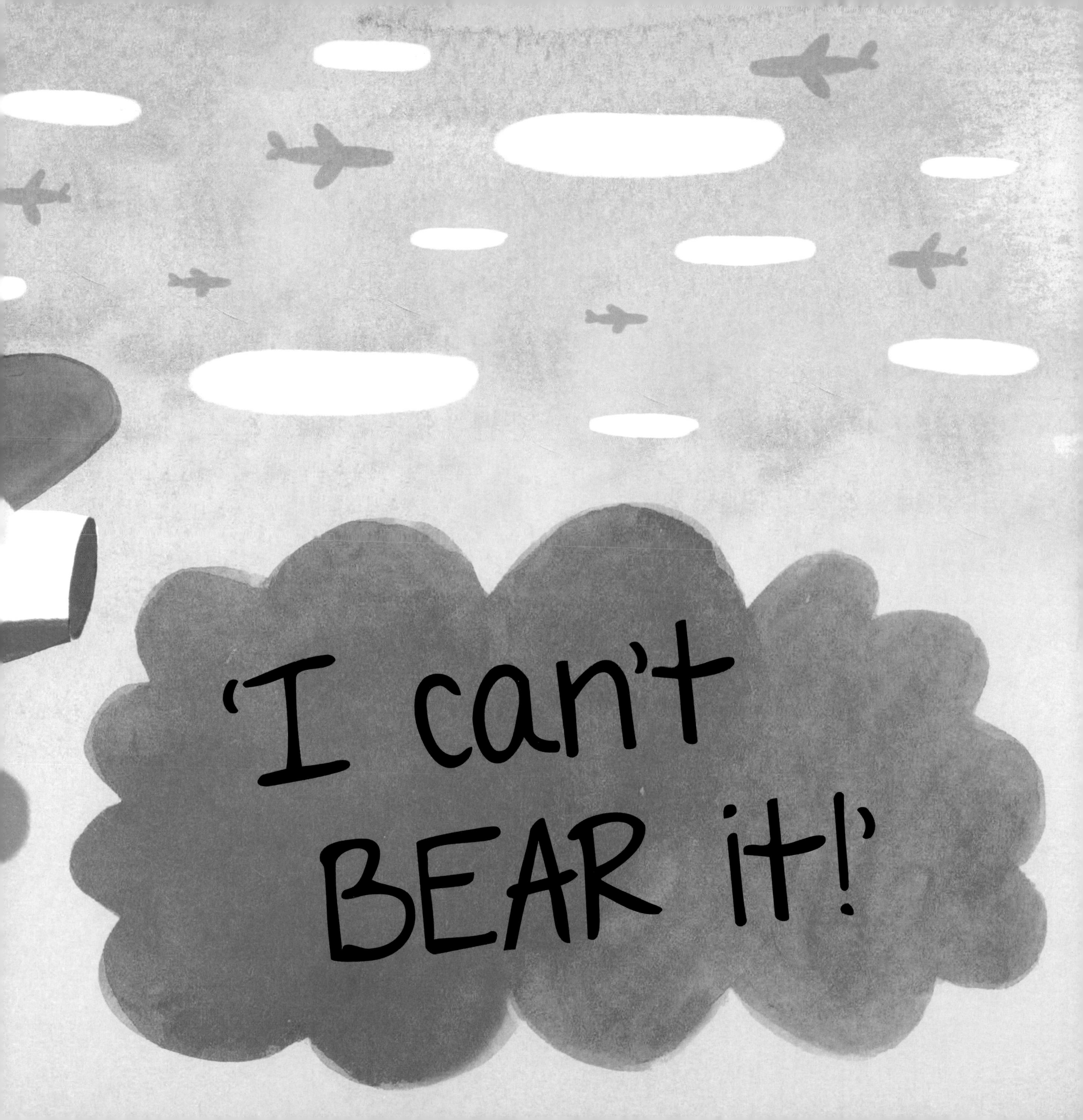
'I can't BEAR it!'